# DANCING WITH LIFE

## TINA LINDEGAARD

Original title: Danser med livet

This book was translated from Danish and edited by
editArt

//MOUSEJOURNAL.COM//

ISBN: 978-87-995568-1-6

Thank you to all of you that I have met in the course of my life. Thank you for teaching me the lessons of life.

Thanks to you, I am the person I am today.

Thank you to all of you that I haven't met yet, and who will help shape the person I will become in the future.

Thanks to you, I will become the person I look forward to meeting.

Or in short:

Thank you to all of you who have given me or will give me the most precious thing in life: The seconds and minutes that will never come back.


And if anyone should wonder: The main character is pure fiction.

# CHAPTER 1

Her eyes catch the first snowflakes that blend with the movements of the wind. Soon the whirls of snow dance like light veils outside the window. She bends forward and rests her elbows on the white windowsill. She feels a slight cold from the window, but the living room is warm, and she can still smell the tomato soup and the bread she toasted earlier in the evening. She watches how the snow, that has now worked its way through the maze of the wind, stains the asphalt. She can see her own reflection in the dark window, but has no time to dwell on it for long before a sound catches her attention. A car door slams with a surprisingly loud noise in the white world outside. Then the cat's nose touches her cheek looking for love and attention.

Almost automatically, her hand strokes the cat's head before it grips the handle of the mug and her attention returns to the cold surface of the window.

Only this time she doesn't look at the snow. Instead she searches out her own reflection. At first glance the reflection looks strange and unknown, and she almost jumps when she slowly recognizes herself. She becomes aware of the smell of coffee. The lines in her face are deeper than she remembers. The dark hair is a little tousled around her face. The reflection seems remote and a little sad to her. The cat's eyes meet hers in the window and for a while they seem locked in each other's search. She puts the cup down again, but that little moment of inattention has unlocked the cat's eyes from hers. This results in another little push from its nose. She smiles as she looks at the cat and lets her hand glide over its head and continue down its back. The cat slightly closes its eyes and clearly enjoys her repeated movements. Slowly it begins to purr – a quiet sound at first, but growing gradually louder.

"What if I had known what I know today? What if I had had that knowledge earlier in life?"

She has not taken her eyes off the cat as she speaks. It sits there quietly with eyes half-closed, just receiving, while it keeps on expressing its pleasure loudly.

"How many mistakes do you think I could have avoided? Hmm – and how many do you think I would have made anyway? It's as if I keep repeating my mistakes over and over again – and it even surprises me every time."

Slowly she stands up, moving her shoulders up and down. She moves her head from side to side and then back and forth. She touches the muscles in her neck and seems satisfied with the result, so she stops. She looks at the amazing dance of the snow in front of her window once more. Every time the flakes are caught in the light of the street lamps, they shine as if they're blinking. They whirl into the oblivion of the darkness, only to turn up in the light again with a new beauty. She smiles to herself and turns away. She thinks. For a long time, she stands completely still before she almost imperceptibly shakes her head. Then she walks over to the living room door where she suddenly stops. A smile spreads over her face as she reaches for the top shelf of the bookcase.

"I have dusted you so many times without ever really relating to you."

Her eyes follow the notebook with its orange plastic cover as she takes it down from the shelf. She notices the pattern of the cover and scratches it slightly with her fingernail.

"Look."

She turns to the cat.

"I bought this because I meant to start a diary."

Her finger picks at the corner of the notebook.

"I never started it. I was always too busy."

She looks at the cat still sitting in the window, but it doesn't notice her. Its tail moves from side to side, and she knows that it has seen something interesting in the street. She looks down at the notebook and tilts her head a little. She sighs quietly and walks over to the window to look down into the street, but she can't see what's so interesting. She stays there a little while. The cat's tail rhythmically sweeps over the painted wood of the windowsill – never seeming to stop. There is nothing there. She looks at the cat that still doesn't pay her any attention and tiredly shrugs her shoulders, puts the notebook down and turns out the light as she leaves the living room.

"Bed time, miss pussycat."

The cat turns its head and looks after her as she leaves, before turning its attention back to the street below.

However, it's not long before she hears the familiar thump of the cat landing on the parquet floor. It looks around the living room, sits down and scratches its neck. Finally, everything seems to be OK and it follows her into the bedroom.

# CHAPTER 2

She's standing in front of the window in the living room – dressed only in her pajama pants and a top – her arms around herself and  a coffee cup in one hand. A chill makes her shiver. Overnight, the asphalt has become a white world caught in the first light of morning. Familiar sounds seem strangely absent in this white world. The apartment is quiet. The cat must still be sleeping. The horizon seems threatening with its dark gray clouds catching the blue light from the sky. The clouds are a sign that the sun is just paying a morning visit, and that the air will soon be filled with white dots of snow falling against the asphalt.

The orange plastic cover catches her eye. It seems strange to her – almost frightening. She lets her fingers run over the cover. The small bumps tickle her fingertips. Her gaze runs over the windowsill and there, to the far right against the wooden frame of the window, her eyes spot a pen. She smiles but seems annoyed.

"Well, it's been here for a long time and I haven't put it away."

She puts her coffee down and picks up the pen and the notebook with her right hand before picking up the cup with her left. She walks over to the window and puts down the cup. Then she carefully puts down the notebook and the pen. She makes sure that the pen won't roll over the edge and land on the floor. The sound that it would make seems frightening to her right now. She looks around and, with some difficulty, moves the green armchair over to the window.

Sitting in the chair, she looks out over the rooftops and in the distance she sees the chimneys of the power plant by the harbor. The pillars of smoke rising from two of the chimneys glide slowly with the wind. She listens, but it's still quiet – she can't even hear the neighbors. She looks around the living room with its dark wooden furniture. The white walls need painting. She suddenly notices the absence of knickknacks. The room seems untouched by human life. The cold creeps over her skin as the chills keep coming. She pulls up her feet in the chair and feels how the soft fabric gently caresses them. She puts the cup to her mouth and the steam hits her face. It feels warm, but soon she feels the damp when the steam touches the cool skin of her face.

The coffee is hot and burns her tongue as she sips. Strangely it doesn't bother her, and she sips the coffee again and again. A peculiar feeling of being alive fills her with every sip. Finally, she puts the cup on the windowsill, just as her eyes catch the orange cover and the pen neatly lying beside it. She slowly picks up the pen with her thumb and index finger and studies it. Her eyes wander towards the notebook. She lets her left index finger slide over the orange cover, and the pattern of the plastic tickles her fingertip. She slowly takes the notebook, puts it in her lap and opens it. She stares for a long time at the blank page, which shines a faint light over her face.

*Dear child*

*You were born into the world of your parents, into their reality. You inherited innocence and your openness, but not necessarily the love within your heart. That must be given to you as a present.*

*You live your first years at the mercy of others. Your open mind takes it all in and stores the memories – both good ones and bad. They're all stored for later use... some would call them experience. You don't judge anyone... not until later in life.*

*But you're destined to lose your openness as your experience deepens. As you get to know the world. Slowly, your innocence fades. You're still young when it begins. It starts slowly. Small actions and words anticipate what your experience tells you will happen if you don't do something. Your openness and your innocence start to feel like a burden, not like something joyful or natural. It's terrible that it has to* be this way, but the world is not an easy place to find your way in – or a safe place for an open and sensitive soul. Little by little, the actions and words become normal, and you're told not to be so sensitive...

... and that the school is a master no one forgets. A master no sensitive soul can survive – a master willing to tear your soul to pieces and leave you to pick them up. But no matter how hard you try, it will never be as fine and pure, open, and innocent as it once was. The scars will crisscross it and scar tissue is never as flexible as intact tissue. There will be pieces of the soul missing all together – broken down by time, which never stops for anyone.

Oh, dear child, you walk a difficult path.

In your school years, you're in a place between innocence and a dawning sense of change. Little by little you understand that the meaning of things changes. You hardly notice it. It's like a part of you. But one day a random reaction from the surrounding world is completely unexpected. What has happened in the mean time – and why? A creeping feeling of fear takes you by surprise. But the feeling is so weak that it feels unreal. A fear of what lies ahead of you, as you realize that this reaction won't be the last – a feeling that you don't really belong anywhere –that you're no longer the same person. You feel the need to do something, but it's not clear what you're supposed to do. Or what's about to happen. It feels like your surroundings, your friends, your parents, and your teachers treat you just a little bit differently. But to you nothing has changed – it's everyone else seeing *things differently – incomprehensibly so. Something must have changed. But has it really?*

The pen stops on the paper as the familiar crunchy sound from the cat's feeding bowl reaches her. Her thoughts linger on whether she fed the cat before going to bed the night before, or if she has to get up to feed it.

It's quiet again. She listens, but there are no more sounds. Her eyes rest on the paper and she slowly lifts the pen. Almost imperceptibly, she hears the sound of cat feet approaching, and just a moment later, the cat sits on the windowsill. She wonders if she can really hear the paws on the floor, or if something else tells her that the cat is coming towards her.

She leans forward and lets her hand run over the cat's back. She feels the heat coming from it, and suddenly realizes that the living room is colder than she thought it was. She puts her hand on her left shoulder and feels how cold it is. On the back of her hand, she feels the surprising power of the cold from the window. She picks up the coffee cup and carefully takes a sip. She's disappointed that the coffee is already lukewarm because she left it on the windowsill.

"Ugh! You must be cold from sitting there."

The cat looks at her with empty eyes. Their eyes hardly meet before it looks out the window again. She glances at the window where fine snowflakes have filled the air.

*My child, I can tell you that the world never stops. Just when you think you understand it, it's already changing. Just as you've made plans and think you're about to carry them out, the world has changed and what do you do?*

She shakes her head and smiles.

*To carry out your plans, my child, that's what life is all about. I can't tell you how to live your life. It wouldn't be fair to you. I have the experience – and I also know the ending. I no longer have the innocence and the naivety that make life easy. These are qualities I have lost on my journey through life. My life is now shaped by the fact that my experiences stop me from achieving what I want. If I had chosen differently, chosen other ways out of my problems, my experience would probably have been different. I would then have seen the world in another light, seen other opportunities and made other choices for the future. But my experience is as I've shaped it, and I must live with the consequences of it. Some choices were good, some not. I wish I'd used the openness that was lost on the path through childhood and school. The clear light of hindsight has already made me decide what's right and what's wrong. Maybe there's no right and wrong, maybe it all depends on the choices we make and the point in time we make them. Maybe all choices are right considering what you know and feel at the time. It's not until you know the consequences and have lived through them that you know whether your choice was right or wrong... Maybe you will never know, never having lived with the consequences of the choices you didn't make.*

*Maybe I failed to live out my choices by continuing down the path I saw in front of me at the time... But why were the other paths hidden from me at the time? When I look back, I see all of them clearly – very clearly, actually*

She puts down the pen. Outside the snowflakes keep on dancing, and all at once the world seems to stop. No sounds. The flakes keep on dancing as they mercilessly cover the world outside, transforming it into a white and cold place. It's as if this white world moves in slow motion. In the street, people walk by slowly – as if time itself has slowed down.

"Hmm."

She leans towards the cat and whispers.

"Do you think the world can stop and still change?"

She stares into the coffee cup, and after a while she carefully puts her finger into the cup.

"Ice cold."

She slowly gets up and leaves the room. Behind her she hears the cat landing on the floor. She smiles.

"So you're hungry after all."

Her voice is teasing as she smiles and looks back at the cat following her. And then their shadows are gone from the door and disappear down the hallway.

The next time she picks up the notebook, it's already dark. She holds it in her hand without really feeling it. Her eyes are on the snow that has formed a ledge against the window. But her gaze is empty. She doesn't see how the top of the ledge has melted from the heat of the window and has formed small frozen streams. To her, the scenery on the other side of the window is a white, blurred mass, and her thoughts are elsewhere. Her eyes are tired and she puts down the notebook in the window, and absentmindedly scratches the cat behind its ear.

"What a day."

She breathes heavily and ends with a snort.

"I can't believe I spend my life doing this. But of course it's making a living – actually a little more than that."

A smile spreads over her tired face.

"Sometimes I just don't know why I do it!"

She looks down at the cat – still smiling.

"And you don't really care, do you?"

She leans down and kisses the cat between the ears.

"Why not just go to bed and read. I'm simply worn-out for today. Do you want to come?"

She picks up the cat and hugs it. For a long time, she holds it close, absentmindedly stroking its head. Without stopping the movement of her hand, she slowly walks across the living room floor.

"Let's go to bed."

# CHAPTER 3

It's still dark when she's back in the living room door. Sleep is still clinging to her body. She puts her arms around herself and rubs her upper arms with her hands. She shudders, as her arms slowly get warm. She stands there and listens, but the silence tells her that the neighbors are not up yet. She sighs into the dark living room, and her eyes glide over the silent, snow-covered rooftops. Her eyes catch the white edge at the bottom of the window. She approaches – her eyes again wandering over the rooftops. When she reaches the window, she looks down into the street. The snow in the traffic lanes has gone and the edge of the snow is now dirty from the splashing of the cars that have passed by in the night. Suddenly it seems like a shame that the simple beauty of the white cover has been sullied, and that it's no longer a perfect whole. On the other hand, she knows that it will make her day and getting to work much easier. She turns her eyes to the bottom of the window, as if she suddenly remembers the reason why she walked over there. Her eyes wander from one end of the frame to the other and then return to where they started. She notices the clear streams of frozen water and leans forward a little. She instantly feels the cold against her face – almost as if a cold hand has lovingly touched her skin. She shivers and pulls away. As she looks in wonder at the window, she slowly reaches her hand out as if to confirm the feeling. Again she feels the cold that quickly wraps itself around her fingers one by one. Then her entire hand is touched by the cold – like a glove surrounding it. She feels the small hairs on her arm stand up as the shivers run over her body incessantly. She takes a step back, shakes her head and quickly rubs her hands against each other. She moves her shoulders up and down to get warm again. She looks around and is once again aware of the silence. She wraps her arms around herself again and squeezes herself tight. Then she leaves the living room.

"Sleepy head – still asleep."

Her voice disappears into the kitchen and becomes remote.

About an hour passes before there's movement in the living room again. The cat struts through the room while licking its mouth. A bit of cat food betrays it. Boldly, it jumps up on the windowsill – then looks attentively out the window before seemingly losing interest in the city outside again. Its body twitches as it sneezes and then shakes its head. Once again, its body becomes rigid as if another sneeze is coming. But, as steps approach, it seems to lose its purpose and turns around attentively.

"There you are. Looks like you've had a good night's sleep."

The smell of perfume reaches its nose as her hand glides over its back. Her eyes follow the hand as if she's scrutinizing that particular part of her body. She sees the notebook and frowns. Almost dreamlike, she opens it. The cover tickles the palm of her hand and, bent over the windowsill, she starts writing.

*Dear teenager*
*I wish I had your body and all the opportunities you have without knowing it. Just think of what you can accomplish if only you try hard enough.*

*I wish you will take care of yourself, so you won't get so many wrinkles later in life.*

She stops and laughs before the pen swiftly passes over the paper.

*~~I wish you will take care of yourself, so you won't get so many wrinkles later in life.~~*

She rests her hand on the cat's head and smiles.

"I guess I have looked too closely in the mirror this morning."

The laughter is still in her voice. She kisses the cat

on the head.

"I think it's about time I get to work. Have fun and don't break too many of my things while I'm gone."

As she winks at the cat, she walks quickly over the parquet floor – her high heels clicking hard against it. Her steps disappear down the wooden stairs of the staircase, and once again the living room is silent. Her steps stop for a moment, but then continue. When she opens the door to the street, the wind is sucked inside.

"Oh!"

Her voice is distant, but her surprise evident.

There is a loud crash from the apartment next door, followed by the sound of breaking glass – and then the sound of a baby crying fills the silence. The sound reaches the cat, and it turns its right ear towards it without moving its head. Soon the sound is no longer interesting, even though it continues for a while.

The sun breaks through the clouds, and the snow looks like stars in the sky as the wind sweeps it over the rooftops. The rays of the sun move across the room as the day passes. The dark furniture seems less robust in the daylight, and the sunlight mixes with the reflection from the wood. It creates an almost golden light in the room. The cat lies stretched out in the window. It looks as if it's dead, but from time to time it moves a little to find a better position in the sunlight.

The orange color of the notebook lights up as the

sunlight glides over it, but fades as the light disappears. When the sun is hidden behind a cloud and doesn't return, the darkness crawls from the horizon into the living room where it settles heavily. The only thing interrupting the darkness and the silence is when the cat walks over the parquet floor – its claws making small, almost unreal little sounds.

The street lights are lit and the furniture casts shadows over the golden floor. The shadows form unrecognizable shapes that settle over the furniture. Lazily, the cat lifts its head and listens before it jumps down and walks sleepily into the hallway. It sits down in front of the door in the dim light that has finished its journey through the living room, and which now settles on the pale wooden floor of the hallway.

The steps on the stairs become more distinct. They move slowly. Finally, she puts the key in the door and the cat gets up.

"Hey you!"

She talks to the cat in a cheerful and light voice while putting down her bags. But her posture and the dark rings under her eyes tell a different story.

"Have you been sleeping? You seem sleepy… or lazy maybe?"

She smiles and strikes the cat's head while closing the door behind her – listening for the sound of the lock.

"Time for dinner. Let's go."

The cat gets up, but she stops.

"Now, look at that!"

She looks down on the pale wooden floor and takes off her shoes. They have left a mark. She shakes her head and steps forward, opens the cupboard and takes out a floor-cloth. She squats and wipes away the dark, salty prints.

"I just don't know why I had to have light wooden floors right here where you enter with your dirty shoes. Not a very bright idea!"

She shakes her head and looks over at the cat sitting next to her, following her every little move. Suddenly there's a paw on the cloth – a single claw is caught in the weave so she can't move it. She smiles and scratches its head, and the paw disappears again. She gets up and throws the cloth into the cupboard and then closes it carefully.

"Come on. Let's get you something to eat."

She picks up her bags, and walks down the hallway with the cat close behind her.

Before long she switches on the light in the living room and heads for the coffee table where she puts down the tray with food. She turns on the TV and settles down in front of the tray and starts to eat. She changes the channel several times while eating. When she's done, she pushes the tray away and moves to a corner of the sofa where she starts zapping again. "Hmm", she says as she looks around for the cat. But she can't see it anywhere.

"Coffee."

She sends out the word into the empty room. She looks around before picking up the tray and getting up. Her steps disappear down the hallway.

"Oh, you haven't finished eating yet. That's not like you."

The sound of wood against wood seems unnaturally loud when she puts down the tray on the kitchen table. Sounds from the china when she puts it in the dishwasher, water from the faucet, and the rustling sounds she makes as she gets the coffee machine ready, follow each other rapidly. She moves across the floor and walks straight to the window.

"I thought so."

She sounds surprised when she leans closer to the kitchen window. The cat has followed her and rubs against her leg. She smiles as she bends down.

"Come on."

Carefully, she picks up the cat and tickles its stomach with a gentle expression in her eyes. She walks slowly down the hallway and over to the window in the living room.

"Have you seen how much snow has fallen since I came home? The cars are hardly moving. I think I could walk faster than that."

She stops in front of the window with the cat in her arms – rocking quietly back and forth. The cat starts to move and she looks down at it – still rocking back and forth. She stops, walks over to the sofa, and picks up the blanket and places it carefully on the windowsill. She moves the small porcelain cat figure, spreads out the blanket a little more and places the cat on it. She watches as it cheerfully walks in circles on the blanket. A snorkeling sound reaches them when the coffee machine announces that it needs cleaning and that the coffee is ready.

"Now you can look outside while I get the coffee."

The cat stops and looks at her when she leaves the room. Then it turns its attention to the world outside which has gone slow and quiet as the snowflakes keep falling heavily.

Carefully, the cat sniffs at the hot coffee that she has placed beside it. The nose vibrates slightly before it pulls away and settles down close to the wall. The room is silent. There is a weak sound of the neighbor emptying the dishwasher, but otherwise it's quiet. Several times, she shifts her weight from one leg to the other. She seems troubled and impatient. She turns away from the window and looks around the room. Then she spots the notebook. Its orange color sticks out from the rest of the room. She looks at it for a long time before picking it up.

"Hmm."

The sound makes the cat open its eyes, but because she isn't moving, it closes them again and goes back to sleep.

She picks up the pen and looks behind her before sitting down – as if to make sure the chair is empty.

She opens the notebook and the words she wrote this morning before leaving the apartment stare back at her.

*Dear teenager*
*I wish I had your body and all the opportunities you have without knowing it. Just think of what you*

*can accomplish if only you try hard enough.*
*~~I wish you will take care of yourself, so you won't~~*
*~~get so many wrinkles later in life.~~*

She looks at the crossed out line and involuntarily makes a face. She runs her hand over her face before putting down the notebook and leaving the room. The click when she turns on the light in the bathroom makes the cat open one eye, and then it jumps down to join her. The crunchy sound of its paws against the cat litter seems refined, and when it once again moves across the floor of the living room, it shakes its paws – spreading cat litter all over the floor. Content, it jumps onto the windowsill and turns around a couple of times before rolling up comfortably and closing the eyes.

Slow steps cross the floor – her breathing sounds like small sighs. She lets herself fall into the chair, but this time the cat doesn't react at all.

*I am wrinkled and vain. Age is in my face – apparent for everyone to see. I look old now – older than I should. All these years, I have forgotten to look in the mirror. I mean, really look at MYSELF in the mirror. Not just at the inner image I have of myself – but at my real, outer image. Why do we trick ourselves?*

She tightens the muscles in her face, and her veins stand out clearly as she clenches her teeth.

*I have been so blind! Only seen what I wanted to see, and only seen in others what I wanted to see. I never saw them for what they really were on the inside. It was probably easier that way, but also emptier than it had to be, I guess. I must have missed getting to know so many wonderful people because I didn't see them for what they were on the inside – maybe I just didn't take the time. Maybe I didn't have the time – or is that just another excuse? Maybe I just don't know how – maybe I have always been too scared...*

*Too scared of situations I couldn't control – situations unknown to me. Maybe I should have sought out just these situations instead of avoiding them.*

Her finger seeks her eyes and removes the tears. But her eyes don't leave the words of this morning. She is angry, shakes her head and passes her right hand over her mouth in a swift movement.

*Dear teenager*

*Take care of your body – it will follow you as long as you live. Don't smoke, like I did when I was your age. Exercise and eat well. You have to live with your body all of your life. Follow all of the dietary guidelines, and get your sleep – at least seven hours every night. Remember switching to cold water when you finish your shower to keep your skin supple. Remember to drink lots of water and stay away from alcohol. And whatever you do – no drugs!*

Her breathing sounds like heavy sighs, and the cat stares at her continuously.

*I used myself up, slept too little, worked too much. And what did I get out of it? A used up body and a used up life...*

*I'm not sure if I regret anything. You can't regret having had fun, having achieved something and having felt like you made a difference. Still, it sometimes seems empty, hollow and not at all what the magazines at the hairdressers write about. It's as if I'm from another age than the one setting the standards now. As if I was born outside of everything. Still, I'm happy with what I have – what I am – even if it came with a price.*

*It was easy to get a boost of energy, so I could deal with more and party some more – easier to relax afterwards with the smoke. But nothing comes without a price. It cost me – and the price was to be paid over a long period of time. A very long time – a time where you watch friends become more and more addicted, slowly, almost unnoticeably. But one day, all of a sudden, it's obvious. Suddenly, one day, you're standing over a grave.*

She puts her arms around herself and strokes them in a hard embrace. She stares at the letters and moves her head back and forth in very small movements.

"How the letters dance! That can't be right."

Suddenly she realizes that the cat is watching her. She looks up at it and it blinks. Then she turns her focus back to the letters, but this time her eyes roam the pages – seemingly unable to settle. Again, she looks over at the cat, and again it blinks at her. Then she holds her breath for a while and looks down – moving the pen back and forth in her hand. Surprised, she stops as a weak sound reaches her. She tenses up, but relaxes as soon as she recognizes the snoring of the cat. Her eyes stay tenderly on the cat for a while, before she grabs the pen and puts it to the paper.

*Dear teenager*
*You have your life ahead of you. Live it your way. Live it so you're happy every day. Life is too short to live it the way others want you to. Live it on your terms.   Enjoy it – every second of it. And never look back. The choices you make are your choices. Maybe they're not always the right ones when you look back at them. But they were the right ones at the time. If they're wrong, change them as soon as you can. Don't wait until you look back at them with bitterness. Then it'll be too late. Then you have let bitterness enter your life – and you don't want that. Let it be for others, but not for you.*

*Don't expect anyone to hand you a fabulous life. Everyone has an agenda that will benefit them and not you. There are no unselfish people. There might be a few, but you'll only hear about them on the news or in a documentary. Create your own life – but don't expect to be able to do that without hard work, without believing in yourself, or without close ties to the few people you know you can trust. People who you know want what's best for you, and who won't put you down for financial gain or to boost their own ego. Be careful; learn before you are grown up, because then the time for learning is over. You'll know when the time is over. It's when, suddenly, unexpected things hurt much more than you can imagine now.*

She snorts.

*Someone once said that life's a bitch! Well, yes it is. But you must learn to love it. It's the only one you'll get!*

She closes the notebook so hard that the cat suddenly stops snoring. It stares at the notebook as she lets it fall into the chair. She then leaves the room with fast and firm steps. All of this happened as if in one movement. The room darkens and the cat stares after her while her shadow disappears down the hallway. But soon the cat is no longer interested and starts snoring gently and slowly again.

# CHAPTER 4

The sound of the snowplow early in the morning blends with the sounds from the kitchen. But the light stays off in the living room. The front door slams behind her. Her running steps on the stairs soon disappear, and then the door to the street closes with a bang.

Several times during the day, the sound of the snowplow is heard, and every time the cat jumps up in the window to see what is happening. Soon the light disappears. The cat sniffs at the half empty coffee cup, but stays put on the blanket from the night before. Silence fills the room, and only the regular, rhythmic breathing of the cat can be heard.

Slowly, the room is filled with sounds as the different people in the building return home. Music is coming from the neighbor and the bass is very clear with deep, resonating vibrations. The breathing of the cat becomes irregular and soon it leaves the room. Before long, you can hear the sound of the food bowl as the cat pushes it over the floor. But nothing happens and the cat moves slowly and returns calmly to the living room. It sits down on the floor, then jumps up in the chair, rolls up and rests its face in its paws. The sound of the bass disappears and the neighbor's door closes – vanishing steps are heard and then the slamming of the street door. Silence returns and a weak snoring from the chair is the only sound.

The cat doesn't hear the quick steps on the stairs before the key is in the lock and the door opens. It sits up in the chair abruptly, but doesn't have time to jump down before she's standing next to it – putting down her bags filled with paper. She quickly moves the cat over to the windowsill without stroking it, and leaves it to stare at her as she sits down in the chair with the notebook. One of its paws hits the coffee cup and some of the cold coffee spills over and forms a small puddle on the wooden windowsill.

*Dear twenties*

*Amazing twenties – when the body is young and the mind still has its innocence – an innocence that bothers you. The insecurity of your childhood lurks just underneath the surface, but a long line of delaying tactics hide it, while you keep telling yourself that you're grown up and in control. What will you do with your twenties? Do you want to waste them on parties? Do you want children and a perfect family?*

*Or have you already planned everything: first your education, then a career and finally kids when you're in your thirties? Do you want to be a free spirit, letting the wind guide you while you wait for what life may bring you? Or will you soar high above life waiting to find the one pot of gold beneath, that'll get you the kind of life dreams are made of? Will you fly full of strength and resolution with the winds of your career – in spite of the sudden winds that'll catch you every time you're not protected by the norms?*

*What do you want? The choice is yours!*

She stops, gets up quickly, and takes the bags into the kitchen. The cat jumps down and follows her, but it's having a hard time keeping up with her. Fast sounds are coming from the kitchen. The china is noisier than usual and the sound of the doors as they are opened and closed is much louder than normally. The sounds from the coffee machine indicate that the coffee is almost done, but the sound won't have time to stop completely before she's back at the chair with a steaming cup of coffee. Absentmindedly, she reaches out and switches on the old, faded floor lamp that swings from side to side when she lets it go. She looks down at the notebook. Then she sits down and places the book in her lap and the coffee on the windowsill. She finally sees the cup from yesterday and the little puddle that has stained the wood. The sounds from the coffee machine stop.

*What will you do with the beginning of your adult*

*life?*

A smile spreads over her face and the light catches a new shine in her eyes – they look happy and a little cunning.

*Oh, the parties were fabulous! Feeling desired, admired, and wanted. I felt beautiful even with a hangover in a pair of old jeans, an oversize sweater, and my hair a mess. Just because I was alive, I got attention from the world around me. Life seemed to last only from party to party. The men came and went and I didn't even find it strange. I would meet a new one the next evening at the next party. Everything kind of flowed together – a collection of memories, of color, lights, music, and happy people – but also physical discomfort in the days after.*

*We were always together in a group – I was never alone. Either we girls were together, some boyfriend or other, or else we were the usual gang. We almost knew each other too well and knew just which buttons to push. No one could drop their front.*

*But, at the same time, it was a continuation of my childhood where my parents were always there. I was never alone. I was surrounded by familiar faces, by safety – or a form of safety. Why should I not wish to feel safe? I just didn't want that feeling from my parents – not anymore. But from people I thought I could trust.*

A crooked smile spreads around her mouth.

*But you can't feel confident that others won't hurt you or put you down. A group like that is almost like a family... You don't fight back, no matter how much it hurts. It's as if the bullying from school follows you into your twenties, but you don't rebel and you don't turn your back on the group. You stay and put up with it. It's as if, in your twenties, you're still just a teenager. In any case, you don't react the way an adult would.*

*It was a hard time – too many parties, too much emotional turmoil. The loss of my parents, and people around me with no understanding of what I was going through. My mind couldn't keep up, and there were too many easy solutions around me.*

*The only thing I really needed was for my body and soul to be in the same place at the same time.*

She breathes hard while absentmindedly scratching her nose.

*Well, there were also the failures, of course. I never got the man I really wanted. I wonder if he would've been worth it. Was it worth getting so down about? I don't know. I thought at the time that he was everything I wanted. Everything!*

*Hmm, I wonder how things would have worked out if we had stayed together. Would we have lived happily ever after, would we have grown apart or would we just have gotten used to each other, so that everything would have become a gray mass or an explosion of color? Would we have gotten along, or did we just think that we would? I didn't really want to get married. I believed that marriage meant chaining down something beautiful. I believed that if it didn't last without the paperwork, it wouldn't last with it. He had another opinion. He wanted all the normal stuff: Marriage, a house, two cars, two children – a boy and a girl – and a labrador retriever – black. That was too much for me in my twenties... it was the complete opposite of the life I was living. How could I even think that he... was the one? I don't get it – and how could he think I was the only one for him...? But then of course I wasn't.*

*I wonder if my heart had actually seen the light in him – known what I really needed and wanted me to have it?*

"Oh, why do I torture myself like this?"

Her outburst makes the cat restless. She notices, but doesn't react.

*What will you do with your twenties? Will they be the start of your future, or are they just for fun?*

She abruptly closes the notebook and takes a sudden sip of her coffee – making a face when she feels the hot steam against her face. She vaguely remembers pouring the coffee, but the thought disappears as soon as it arrives. She stares angrily at the notebook. Her gaze is firm and her body locked in an awkward position – halfway turned away from the notebook. Slowly she opens it.

*The twenties are wonderful and terrible at the same time – wonderful because of all the opportunities ahead of you, but terrible because of your lack of experience. The wrong choices are so easy to make, and they have no consequences until much later in life. Nothing is ever without consequences – they're always there. Sometimes you're lucky and feel them right away – sometimes they're completely invisible until they suddenly upset your life completely. They're waiting for you – like a spider, they wait patiently until you're caught in their web – and then it's too late.*

*If only life came with a patient package insert! Think before you say yes. Think about what will happen if you don't! Just think!*

*Life comes without right of revocation! You can't take it back or swap it for something new. What's done can't be undone. You can't erase other people's memory and you cannot always remove what's sick – it so often comes back. No one is immortal, and life is no Hollywood movie – always ending happily, no matter how impossible things have become on the way. The reality of life is there every morning when you open your eyes. If you go away, your memories will follow. If you numb yourself with all the drugs you can find, reality will hit you every time they stop working. You can't escape the prison of life – you're born into it and will die in it. It's as if everything happens with small, insignificant steps that we hardly*

*notice. It happens minute by minute – step by step –*
*and suddenly we live the consequences.*

She looks at the words for a long time – feeling
empty. Her body seems stooped and the wrinkles
and lines in her face show clearly in the faint, yellow
light from the floor lamp – seeming stronger from
being the only light in the room. The yellow light
makes her look sick – like an old woman, bent over
in her chair – just waiting. She suddenly realizes how
much her tongue still hurts from the scalding coffee
and how it creates a gritty feeling in her mouth.

*Now is the time to write something encouraging,*
*something that will give you hope, something that will*
*make you look forward to your thirties – something*
*that will make you love life and make you continue*
*happily down life's highway – birds singing above you.*
*I have to think carefully – of course life is worth living*
*– of course I love life – or else I wouldn't still be here –*
*or would I?*

She carefully drinks from her coffee cup, now
finally without any steam – her eyes slowly looking
around the living room. They don't seem to
recognize anything. She gets up and stands in front
of the window with her arms folded in front of her.
Her breathing is deep, but gradually gets lighter and
shallower – ending in something resembling thrusts
– and she slowly removes one tear after another from
her cheek. She puts the notebook on the windowsill

and, still hunched over, she continues writing.

*Life is like a never ending love story. You get some blows from time to time, but good things make up for them. We are fortunate enough to remember all the good things that happen to us, while the bad things seem to lose their power – a little every day. Maybe we walk through life without reflecting very much, and when we do, we don't really do anything about it. You can't stop and rewind to the point where you know afterwards that you should have chosen differently. Maybe we live instinctively from breath to breath not knowing any better... or not wanting to know better...*

She carefully removes the tears that have fallen down on the paper with her fingertips. The paper swells as the moist penetrates its structure. Her eyes dry out, and she slowly realizes how gritty they feel. She leaves the notebook lying open, takes her coffee cup, and turns off the lamp on her way out. She stops in the door and closes it behind her – leaving it just a little open for the cat. Silence returns and soon the ray of light on the living room floor is also gone.

# CHAPTER 5

The night is quiet – only interrupted by the sound of the alarm clock, which she quickly switches off. The door remains half closed, and her voice can be heard from time to time – talking to the cat. Her voice is light and seems playful and frivolous. She plays with the cat in the kitchen, accompanied by the sound of the coffee cup that she puts down on the counter from time to time. Then she opens the front door and the sound of her fast steps drowns in the sound of the street door closing. Some minutes pass before the cat plods into the living room and heads straight for the windowsill. It stops briefly before it sets off and lands on the blanket. Kneading the blanket with its paws, it turns once before balling up on the blanket. It falls asleep right away. Slowly, the light crawls through the window as the sun rises, and soon the living room fills with a sunlight, that only brings with it the warmth of winter.

The cat wakes up several times during the day and disappears through the half closed door. At one time, you can hear the sound of cat litter under the cat's paws – and at another time, the sound of the food bowl being pushed over the floor. As the light slowly fades, the cat is fully awake again – attentively following the movements in the street. It suddenly jumps down from the windowsill and hurries through the living room into the hallway. The sound of paws on the wooden floor stops at the front door. Shortly after, the sound of the door to the street can be heard as it closes, and steps on the stairs become unmistakable.

She hums as she puts the key in the lock.

"Oh, you're waiting for me."

The bags stretch and creak under the weight of her shopping. The cat makes a faint sound as she lifts it up – as if the air is being pushed out of its lungs.

She mumbles faintly to the cat, moving around the apartment, until finally she's in the living room with the cat in her arms – her head against its head. The cat purrs and looks content to be touched. She sits down in the green armchair without letting go.

"You're so soft and warm – so wonderful to touch. You want me to put you down?"

Her hand strokes its head.

"Oh, you want to sit in the window? Here you go."

She holds the cat over to the windowsill where it leaves her arms. She gets up from the chair and looks over the cat's head down into the street. Then she bends down and kisses it on its head. She leaves the room, and the sound of the creaking plastic bags is heard again when she disappears into the kitchen.

Shortly after, the sound of the food bowl makes the cat jump down and walk into the hallway.

Some time passes before the cat comes back with her right behind it. It doesn't stop, but jumps straight onto the windowsill.

"How was the food?"

She bends over the cat and lets her hand run across its head. Continuing, she picks up the open notebook while kissing the cat on its head and falling into the armchair.

The pages of the book have moved since she left it. Now a blank page stares back at her. She smiles and her gaze lingers on the blank page for a while, before she flicks back through the pages. She quietly reads while thinking.

Her eyes are stuck to the page, as she reads the same sentence over and over again:

*Don't expect anyone to hand you a fabulous life.*

She raises her eyes and lets them rest unfocused on the room around her. Then it's as if her eyes come to life again.

*Dear thirties*
*Oh, thirties – how wonderful you are! Your self confidence blooms, your career is running smoothly –*

*and if it's not, panic sets in. So hope that it is! You're slowly beginning to figure out who you really are, and it's as if the world is opening up to you.*

*But the start of the thirties is terrible. The norms of society hit you hard. When are you getting married and starting a family? If you haven't heard that yet, you will – unless you follow the norms and get married and start a family soon. It really doesn't matter if you're divorced three years later. Then you'll just be like all the other single, divorced parents. You'll have something to talk about at family reunions. You'll also be one of the sad ones. Oh, yes – the norms are alive and well, and a lot of people live by them without even thinking about it. The worst thing about the thirties, is that the insecurity of youth still lurks in the back of your mind, and you know deep down that it'll turn up when you least want it to. It'll come as a surprise every time you get that sinking feeling in your stomach. Right then and there, you know that it's the insecurity playing a trick on you. Norms and insecurity... it's a lethal cocktail, my friend. Take care of yourself.*

*When you have learned not to bother about it, and you have finally said no to your oldest aunt – noticing the way the corners of her mouth turn downwards. When she still isn't convinced that you don't have some secret disease no one has heard of, or, a thought that she tries desperately not to think: that maybe you're gay – that's when you'll realize how great the thirties actually are. The thirties are a good time.*

*Would I have done anything differently? Would I*

*have been more focused on a specific part of my life or maybe just a few – instead of focusing on everything the way I did…?*

She smiles and blinks a couple of times – keeping her eyes on the paper.

*I don't really know… It's as if life has been something alive and dynamic – just evolving – independently from me. Life has had a life of its own. I have just tagged along – opportunities and developments happening on the way. I seized some opportunities when they happened, and was carried forward just by being in the right place at the right time. I didn't really help create the opportunity – it was just suddenly there. Then it was time to do the right thing at the right time – that took some work. But I succeeded. Some other things just wouldn't work, though – no matter how hard I tried. But I guess that's the nature of life. Sometimes it's easy to succeed at something – other things require hard work. And then there are the things you just never succeed at – no matter how hard you work – or how much you plan. Hmm, is luck really necessary to succeed?*

*If only I knew where Lady Luck lives, I would camp out on her doorstep until she promised me eternal luck.*

She smiles.
"If only I could do that."

Her eyes rest on the window pane reflecting the light in the room against the dark sky outside.

*Is Lady Luck really someone I don't know? Is she such a stranger to me? OK, I have been in the right place at the right time. Then some buttons needed pushing, and then it worked out. Is that luck, or did I create it?*

"What do you think?"

She looks at the cat and again she strokes its head. This time it doesn't even bother to lift its head to show that it's happy. It just opens one eye a little. When she removes her hand, the eye closes again and the cat goes back to sleep.

She quickly raises one eyebrow – almost annoyed. Again, her gaze is unfocused – she looks around the room while taking regular, heavy breaths.

*I really don't think I know Lady Luck. I don't even think I would recognize her if I ran into her in the street. I would walk right past her, and if she should whistle at me, I would get angry and ask her what she thinks she's doing!*

"So much for being open."

She sighs and looks away.

"I really don't think that I'm very open to life."

She puts down the notebook.

"Well, I need some coffee. Would you like some food?"

The cat listens attentively to her, and when she leaves the room, it hurries after her. The notebook is left behind with two empty pages waiting to be written on. The pen is on top of the pages – keeping the notebook open. Almost imperceptibly, the pen moves and the pages close around it.

Some time passes before suddenly she's standing over the notebook again. In one hand she's holding a slice of white bread with cheese, in the other a cup of coffee. She stares at the closed notebook for a long time without moving. Then she puts down the cup firmly on the windowsill, and struggles a little with the slice of bread that keeps folding over – before putting it down next to the coffee.

*I'm not open to life. I keep looking ahead – trying to predict what will happen, instead of living in the moment. Maybe that's why Lady Luck has always been such a hazy figure. I have always thought that others were lucky, but never me.*

*People say that luck will find you and you shouldn't go looking for it. Well, if that's true, there's a reason I haven't had much luck. I didn't really believe in it, and I still don't. So why am I so worried not to know Lady Luck.*

"Oh, you know what?"

She looks at the windowsill and is surprised not to find the cat there. She looks around, worried, but she can't see the cat anywhere.

"Hmm, where are you?"

She gets up fast and disappears into the hallway, calling the cat's name. Her footsteps can be heard around the apartment.

"Oh, there you are  – already in bed, waiting for me. But I won't be coming to bed for a while. You're so sweet – all sprawled out on the bed."

Walking briskly, she's back in the living room again. She picks up the coffee cup and feels it. Then she disappears out the door again.

"What, you haven't eaten everything?"

The food bowl makes a noise when she puts it back on the floor.

"Oh, how stupid I am!" I have already fed you once after I came home. Well, then you must be full. Maybe that's why you've already gone to bed."

Her steps are heard in the bedroom.

"Full and feeling good?"

She comes back with the coffee cup, but this time the coffee is clearly hot. She sips it and makes a face.

"Man, that's hot."

She picks up the cheese sandwich and starts eating – very slowly and carefully. Her face is calm and thoughtful.

She eats for a long time, all the while sipping at the coffee frequently. When she's finally done, she gets up and leaves the living room. The sound of the cup hitting the bottom of the sink reaches the living room almost like an explosion, breaking the total silence in there. Shortly after, you can hear the sound of water in the bathroom sink. She drifts into the living room – waving her hands in the air to make

sure they're dry. She lets herself fall into the chair –
still waving her hands. Finally, she rubs them against
each other – satisfied.

*I don't even think I thought about luck in my
thirties. I believed then, that if only I worked hard
enough, I could achieve anything. I didn't want to be
given anything – didn't want anyone to help me. I
thought that in order to enjoy my success, I had to
achieve it by myself – all by myself, even if it meant
working twenty hours every day. I was so sure that
was the only way. But what was success? I think that
for me all progress was success. I was terribly modest
about my ambitions. I didn't want to set my goals to
high, so the defeats wouldn't be too hard to take...*

"Oh, what was I thinking?"
She shakes her head furiously.
"I've been so stupid!"
She gets up and walks over to the door, but stops
suddenly. She turns around and looks back at the
notebook, and then she marches back and throws
herself into the chair.

*Was I really so scared that I couldn't see that forest
for the trees?"*

She doesn't notice, but the cat watches her from
the door. She never looks up and doesn't see the cat
turning around – heading for the bedroom with
determination.

*Promise me that you'll never be scared of life. It's big and wild and fierce. It's exciting and challenging. It's quiet and beautiful. Like the ocean it can suck you down into the cold undercurrent, where you can easily drown. Learn to swim, so you'll never be afraid to be alive – be yourself.*

She snorts and gets up – closing the notebook and throwing it back into the chair. She leaves the room purposefully and her steps take her into the kitchen. Then it's quiet. From time to time her crying can be heard clearly, before the silence takes over again. She turns on the light in the bathroom and blows her nose several times. She walks into the bedroom and everything is quiet once again.

# CHAPTER 6

The next morning, she turns on all the light in the apartment, but the living room is left in darkness. Her steps can be heard all over the apartment, but they never reach the living room. When she closes the front door behind her, the cat slowly shuffles across the living room floor and jumps up in the chair. It circles the notebook a little, before finally lying down with its back resting against it. The apartment is quiet as clear rays of sunlight once again crawl slowly over the floor – finally filling the room entirely. Along with the rest of the room, the chair is filled with the faint winter-warmth of the sun, and the cat stretches and pushes the notebook over the edge of the chair. It lands upside down with the cover forming a kind of protective roof over the creased pages. The cat is lying on its back with its head hanging over the edge of the chair – looking at the notebook. Slowly, its eyes are closing, and it just lies in the chair letting the sunbeams run across its stomach.

When her voice is heard in the staircase, the sun has disappeared a long time ago. Her voice is almost shrill and she talks rapidly. She stops on the floor below – quiet all of a sudden. As she approaches, her voice becomes louder and the words are said with emphasis. She stops outside the front door and puts the key in the lock. The cat is sitting in the chair – tense, and when the door opens, it jumps quickly down and disappears into the darkness of the room. Her bags land heavily on the floor and the door slams hard. She throws her coat through the living room door, where it lands in a bundle on the couch.

"Damn it, it's too much. They can't keep doing that. I thought it was over by now. If I keep working 24 hours a day, I will drop dead before my time."

Her shoes slide noisily over the floor and one of them hits the wall with a loud slam. Then it's quiet. The faucet in the kitchen makes a familiar sound and, soon after, so does the coffee machine. With an explosion of sound, she firmly pulls a chair over the kitchen floor. Then it's quiet. Far away, on one of the other floors, children's feet can be heard running. It's quiet again. The coffee machine makes its familiar sounds – still clearly expressing that it needs cleaning. Long after the coffee machine has stopped, the silence hangs heavily over the apartment.

The soft sound of the cat's paws landing on the

windowsill disappears into the silence. She clatters with the cups in the kitchen. It's as if the cat suddenly realizes that it's evening now and it's hungry again. Quickly it jumps down. The sound of its claws breaks the silence as it hurries into the kitchen.

"Oh, there you are!"

Her voice is calm and level. The rattling sound of the dry food landing in the cat's bowl seems overwhelming compared to the silence resting over the apartment.

"It's so quiet here – it's almost unnatural. It's as if the world has stopped."

She hesitates, almost unbelieving. Then the cat breaks the silence as it happily crunches the dry food. She moves the chair again and soon after she turns on the faucet.

"Here you go – that will last for a while."

The sweetness in her voice is back. The sound from the cat fills the apartment, and then the sound of children's feet running over the neighbor's floor finally breaks the silence completely.

"You want to come into the living room?"

It's like she asked the question too late, because at the same moment, the cat flies into the living room with a toy mouse in its mouth. It makes a show throwing the mouse over the floor and then catching it again before it lies still.

"You're so dangerous."

She follows the cat and the smile is back in her voice. She takes the mouse from the cat and throws it on the couch where it lands in her coat. The cat gets even more excited and it suddenly jumps for the couch – landing head first in the sleeve of the coat.

"Stop, stop."

Her voice is still soft, as she hurries to put the coffee cup down, trying to reach her coat before the cat throws itself around in it again – chasing the disappeared mouse.

"Stop…"

Her voice fades and a small, suppressed laughter fills the oppressive silence following the sound of running children's feet.

"What do you think you're doing? Is it a killer mouse?!"

The cat is throwing itself all over the coat – having caught the scent of the mouse again. The mouse flies through the air abruptly and lands on the floor in front of her feet, but the cat hasn't seen it yet and just sits with its head inside the sleeve of the coat.

"Here, you crazy bastard."

She scratches the wooden floor with her fingernail and slowly the noise gets through to the cat in its fantasy world. It pulls its head out of the sleeve and looks towards the noise. Then it turns to face the mouse, arches its back while tripping with it hind legs, and then suddenly sets off towards the mouse. There's no resistance from the wooden floor and the cat slides elegantly over the floor, over the mouse and into her leg. However, it doesn't seem to bother it much and it jumps to face the mouse again and repeats the entire procedure. This time it catches the mouse before it slides towards the door, and in a huge jump it disappears down the hallway. Soon the rattling sound of the bed sheets can be heard – the cat now attacking the sheets instead of the coat.

She looks at the coat and smiles.

"I can check the damages later."

She looks over at the window. Inquisitively, her eyes search the yellow skies, where the city lights are reflected against the bottom of what looks like another cloud full of snow. After a while she walks up close to the window. Everything is silent once again. Tense, she listens for the slightest sound. Then the sound of the cat slowly approaching reaches her. She turns around and sees a tired cat strutting into the living room with the toy mouse in its mouth.

"Well."

The smile in her voice is unmistakable and the cat seems to pay more attention. She sits down in the chair and the cat comes over and stands in front of her.

"How cute you look!"

Almost automatically, she picks up the notebook and places it open in her lap. The cat blinks and jumps up to her – proudly giving her the wet toy mouse. Soon a wet circle spreads from the mouse onto the paper of the notebook, and the pages crease up in little moist bumps.

"Oh no, where was this mouse? I hope it was the water bowl!"

The entire attitude of the cat is one of pride and her exclamation doesn't seem to affect it. It looks at her, squints, and crawls from the armrest over onto the windowsill where it gets comfortable and directs its attention out over the rooftops.

"Gee!"

Her voice is low and doesn't reflect much awareness of her choice of words.

"I really hope it was the water bowl!"

She removes the toy mouse from the notebook and lets it fall on the floor where it lands with a weird, soft, and round noise. Carefully she pushes it aside with her right toe.

The cat is completely unaware of her efforts to remove the wet toy animal. Instead it circles around itself to find the best place to lie down. It doesn't seem to work, however, and instead it starts kneading the blanket with its front paws. She looks at the cat and waits as it circles again. Only this time it seems to work better. It only takes three rounds before it lies down in one smooth movement.

"I believe in the saying: You must feel an animal with your soul – or you shouldn't have an animal at all."

She shakes her head when she discovers that the cat is already almost asleep – lying there with something resembling a smile on its face. She looks down at the notebook where the paper seems to have stopped creasing.

"What a sorry sight!"

Her words are dry and to the point as she looks at the wet and curled up pages.

"Well, we mustn't let it darken our light minds, as

my dad used to say."

She lets the palm of her hand glide over the pages a couple of times.

"That didn't help much. It was so nice before."

She looks over at the cat – now lying on its back with all four paws in the air. The only answer she gets is a weak snoring.

"OK, I get the hint. You couldn't care less."

A loud snort is the answer to that.

"Yes, yes."

She looks for the pen on the floor and finds it next to the wet mouse.

"Great! Well, at least that isn't wet also."


*Dear forties*

*Something is not right about the forties. For the first five or six years, it feels like time has gone backwards. You feel like you're somewhere in your late twenties to mid-thirties – only more confident. It comes like a bit of a surprise. But you know it's there. Unexpectedly, one day, something feels different. Suddenly you know who you are. Strange feeling – but fabulous!*

*With this awareness comes another one – a very different one. Your goals suddenly become blurry and disappear. Slowly, weak outlines of your future goals appear, and all of a sudden, they're clear as daylight in front of you. It's like you only have to reach out to get them. All you need to do is close your hand around them and pull them close. They're right there in front of you all the time. But then they turn out to be*

53

*incredibly far away – like a mirage trembling in the heat of the desert.*

*At the same time, it's as if something falls into place – as if you suddenly belong in the world – and have a place in it that's all yours. It belongs to you – just the way you are. Not as you could be, or as you should be, but as you are. Your shortcomings, that used to be so important to you, don't really mean anything anymore. You have accepted your body and thus opened up to intimacy, which is suddenly much more present in your life than it used to be. It's a little annoying that this joy comes so late in life.*

She smiles a crooked smile and looks up.

"I wonder if my coat is in one piece."

She tilts her head a little while her eyes remain focused on the coat on the couch. Her thoughts are somewhere else as she closes the notebook – leaving the pen inside as a bookmark before getting up. She heads straight for the coat. She picks it up and takes it with her into the hallway where she switches on the light. The sound of the coat being turned this way and that lasts for a long time. Then she opens the cupboard and the sound of the hanger against the metal bar is loud and clear. With hesitant steps, she walks towards the chair again and sits down quite slowly. She fumbles a little when she tries to open the notebook with the pen. She looks somewhere above the notebook for a while, but finally she looks down and opens the book with a swift movement.

*Who promised me a fabulous life?*

*At least it wasn't fabulous at the end of my forties. A life, which should have carried on my genes after I was gone, was wasted because of ambitions and because I wasn't able to slow down and focus. Like so many others before me, I thought I could do everything at once. He never forgave me, and I still haven't forgiven myself. I thought there was an easy way out of the pain of losing both of them, but I was wrong. The time in hospital and the sessions with the psychologist afterwards helped me see the logic of what happened. But when things really matter to you, you only see with your heart. Only your heart can see clearly. Learn to listen to it – and fast. That will save you a lot of worries. But be prepared. Your heart cannot lie – it's simply not in its nature.*

*So far, I have not been able to forgive myself. How do you forgive yourself for something that no one else can forgive you for? I changed my job to get away... Physically I'm removed from it, but not mentally. I can still remember how it felt physically when it started. I still see the stain on the chair when I got up – and the desks in the common office... Worst of everything, I still feel, over and over, the warm and wet feeling of something moist running down my legs in small streams. They got colder as they ran down my legs – almost a tickling feeling. Even after all this time, the feeling comes back to me every time something lightly touches the inside of my legs. The shocked look on my colleagues' faces – and then they tried to look away or ignore me entirely. No one seemed to remember how they pushed me, or maybe they just didn't want to be confronted with the consequences of their actions. Just as they tried to forget what happened to me in the time leading up to it. It didn't just happen. But it was too late. My daughter came into the world much too soon and had to leave it again – much too soon.*

*She was too small. The doctors couldn't save her. She had dark hair, the finest little fingers...*

The pen stops, but remains pressed against the paper. She holds her breath, and time seems to lose its grip on the present. A muffled gasp escapes her lips, and suddenly the pen moves hastily over the paper.

*Coming back to work was terrible. My colleagues kept their distance, and I didn't feel that they understood what I had gone through. They didn't really want me to talk about it, and probably didn't really want to understand why. My understanding of myself and my interaction with my job broke down when human resources told me that they couldn't understand how I could have let it come to that. That it was my responsibility to stop it. Today, I still wonder what might have happened, if I had slowed down and the deal had dropped. I wonder if they would have fired me...? I think so... or maybe not. I simply don't know, and I'm mad at myself for even thinking it.*

*If they had fired me, I would probably still have my*

*baby. Was that really the choice I was facing? If I had understood that then, would I have chosen differently? Today I know what I would have chosen to do, but it's always so heartbreakingly easy to see the past clearly – while the path ahead is always unclear.*

Her naked ring finger runs up and down the spine of the notebook, but she doesn't look at it. Instead, she looks out in the room with an empty gaze. She gets up and disappears from the room. A cupboard is opened in the kitchen and the water hits the bottom of the sink with a loud noise. Then she slowly returns to the chair. The cat is still snoring happily, and she looks at it – surprised. She stands in front of the window – slowly drinking her glass of water. She shakes her head repeatedly – hugging herself. The changing colors of the sky make the shadows outside change their tone, while the sounds coming from the street change little by little. She slowly lets herself go and finally drinks the last of the water before putting down the glass on the windowsill. This time the sound disturbs the cat in its sleep. It slowly gets up and arches. But as soon as that's done, it lies back down and falls into a deep sleep once again. She watches it for a long time, but the only thing that changes is how deep it breathes. She senses the smell of warm radiator and reaches down under the windowsill to touch it.

"Ouch!"

The cat opens one eye and looks at her with wonder. She looks back at the cat and then down at her hand.

"Well, it's not really that warm in here, so it must be right."

She looks over at the cat that's cleverly working itself into an awkward position – half on its back and with the lower part of its body lying on its side. She tilts her head a little and then walks over to sit down in the green armchair.

*Someone has said that the forties are the new thirties. Yes, yes, absolutely – and how great that feels! In your forties, you live more in the moment, and you have more courage. You're more THERE! You see yourself as an independent being. The moment is huge and exciting. But only if you make good use of it and don't let everyday life take over. You must remember to stop and look at the weather. Stay just a few moments longer in the rain, so you really feel it instead of just establishing that it's raining. Feel with your body and your soul. Taste, smell, and feel. Feel with your fingers and especially with your heart. Only your heart sees your reality.*

*In your forties, you're more at ease with yourself and more extroverted, but at the same time more focused on your inner life. Contemplation becomes a necessity, something you really need to do – a part of yourself you cannot live without. You need your body and your soul to be in the same place at the same time. With that comes the need for romance. Practicalities are a thing of the past... that is, until you need to prepare packed lunches for the kids – and who picks them up and who does the shopping? Oh, the wonderful kids. Even if they're not your own, you still love them. It's a strange feeling... you know you'll lose them if you lose the boyfriend. You have put your heart on the line. The stakes in a relationship are so much higher and you're more careful what you say and do. But romance still wants its share, even if it's reduced to small, affectionate notes in the packed lunch, or a sweet text message at the end of the day: "Hi honey, I'll get the milk on the way home – see you at home."*

*At times you lose yourself in the other person. No one else exists – that is, except your cranky boss – cranky because you chose to go out to dinner with that special person in your life, instead of finishing the spreadsheet that he wanted on his desk at 8 next morning. And just on the one night where the kids are with his ex-wife.*

*The other person becomes your passion. Your body feels warm all day, and you can't wait to get home to kiss this amazing person. Oh, that is such a wonderful time and you must enjoy it to the full. Sometimes everything disappears as if by magic once you get to know the other person. Once you see behind the qualities you have attributed to the person, and start to see the actual person. At first it's only a glimpse – like the sun skipping on the surface of the water. Then these glimpses start to appear more often, and you start paying attention to them – and that's where it starts. Now you see these glimpses every time you see the person. You start to connect them to each other, and you completely forget to forgive the person for not being the person you made up in your head – a person with qualities that have nothing to do with reality. This fabulous person who fulfills all of your needs without you even having to mention them... everything you look for without knowing it. You forget that opposites attract and that you actually want a person who's different from yourself. You start to get annoyed at how difficult everything is, and you start to wonder what kind of person you have actually found – it's almost as if he takes the opposite position just to annoy you. Does he actually love you...? Doubt starts to do its work.*

*Where did the Hollywood story go? Sometimes I wonder if Hollywood just puts silly ideas in everyone's heads, so we end up as frustrated individuals that don't understand why our lives are the way they are. Why don't they resemble the stories that we have always been fed with? Are we really so stupid, that our lives always fail, when they always succeed in Hollywood?*

*Hmm, back to yesterday: DON'T EXPECT ANYONE TO HAND YOU A FABULOUS LIFE – THAT IS YOUR OWN RESPONSIBILITY!*

*Life is no Hollywood movie. No one will come to save you, no one will feel sorry for you and help you, and no one will kill you when everything seems darkest, and free you from you misery... As if that was an option.*

She slowly closes the notebook and looks into the

dark living room – deep in thought. The light from the window and the yellow sky gives one side of her face a dull, spooky yellow gleam. She wets her lips, but her eyes and her body don't move. Slowly she gets out of her cross-legged position and puts her left foot on the floor. Her right foot touches the floor and suddenly she jumps sideways in the chair. Her right foot hovers over the floor as she looks down. Beneath it is the wet toy mouse. She turns her foot over and looks at her sock, where at dark stain reveals that she has stepped on it. She shakes her head and looks over at the cat – now lying with its head deeply buried in its paws and its tale wrapped around its body.

She carefully puts her foot next to the toy mouse and gets up – letting the notebook fall on the chair. She walks over to the cat and puts her head close to it while putting her hand on its back

"You're so bad."

She whispers as the cat slowly opens its eyes and stares into hers with a careful softness. She kisses its head and runs her hand over its back as she moves away from it. When she reaches the door, she looks back at the yellow clouds once again.

"Hmm, looks like it will snow again tonight."

# CHAPTER 7

The night is quiet and soon the first snowflakes fall
on the ground. As the night progresses the frame of
the window is filled with a whirling mass of white
dots – seemingly dancing in front of the glass on
their way towards the sidewalk below. When the
flakes hit the glass, it takes a long time before they
melt. After at while they form little, clear streams as
the surface of the water freezes on its way to the edge
of the window. Late in the night, you can hear the
sound of the street sweepers making their first
rounds, and they have made several before the light
from the kitchen throws its faint beam of light into
the living room. Still drowsy, she walks through the
living room – her hair a mess in the back – as she
holds the bathrobe close to keep warm.

"Gee!"

Her voice is low.

"Gee, it's time to get ready and get out of here.

The bus will be packed."

She shudders and looks around for the cat.

"Ha, she's probably still lying at the foot of the bed."

Her steps are still slow, but she puts her feet to the floor more firmly.

"So you don't want to get out of bed? You can wait until I've showered, then I'll make the bed on top of you. Sleep well."

Her voice is soft and affectionate. With a click, the lights go out, and for a moment the apartment is left in darkness until another click reveals the light from the bathroom. That doesn't last long, though. A small streak of light falls on the wooden floor of the hallway as she closes the bathroom door and soon the sound of water hitting the tile floor fills the silence.

Once again, the street sweepers pass by below the apartment, and soon the sound of water is gone. The cat has stirred its food bowl without achieving anything, and then it slowly walks over behind the armchair. A clear sound of fabric ripping reveals what it's doing.

"STOP THAT!"

Her voice cuts through the silence, and the cat jumps away from the chair – staring at the doorway, scared.

Shortly after she pokes her head into the living room, but the cat is still behind the chair where she can't see it. With wet feet, she walks towards the bedroom. Hurried sounds of doors opening and closing in the bedroom follow before she turns out the light again. She moves around the dark apartment, and then switches on the light in the kitchen and opens the door to the fridge. A chinking sound of glasses follows and then she opens and closes the fridge door again. It's suddenly silent. The cat has discovered where she is and comes running. A rustling – and then the sound of the food bowl being filled, and the cat knows that it has achieved what it wanted.

"Take care, sweetie. How fast you're going!"

She walks quickly over the living room floor and stops in front of the window.

"Oh, it looks even worse now. Wow!"

She moves quickly and turns to leave the room. She notices the notebook and stops abruptly. She stares at it. The orange cover forms a beautiful contrast to the green fabric of the armchair. A faint smell of toast from the apartment downstairs spreads through the ventilation – reminding her how hungry she actually is. She leans forward, her eyes locked on the notebook.

"No no! It will have to wait till I get home."

She shakes her head and leaves the living room with fast and determined steps. A loud sound is heard from the cupboard, her coat makes a rustling sound and soon the door slams behind her.

A faint noise reveals that the cat is moving down the hallway towards the living room, but crunching noises from the cat litter in the litter box show that the living room wasn't its final destination. After a while, its steps can be sensed again, but the sound grows weaker and a new sound mixes with the sounds from the neighbor. The metallic sound from the cat's nameplate on its collar makes a delicate, pure sound every time it hits the water bowl. The sound disappears and the food bowl rattles again. Then it's quiet again and the noises from the neighbors fill the rooms.

Finally, the cat comes strolling through the living room. It jumps up onto the windowsill, and stares in wonder at the white mass of dancing snowflakes preventing it from seeing the rooftops on the other side of the road. It puts back its head and sees only the snowflakes whirling towards it. But before long it loses interest and jumps back down. It stops in front of the armchair. Then it strolls on and disappears from the living room. Soon the sound of cat-cuddling-with-bed-linen spreads in the apartment, and a small content grunt comes from the bedroom, as the cat gets comfortable on the unmade bed.

The day resonates with the sound of the street sweepers and the snowplows passing in turn while it's still light. As darkness settles and drags long shadows over the living room floor, the intervals between the mechanical sounds are longer and then they disappear entirely.

The noise from the cars becomes louder and finally steps are heard in front of the door. The cat lands on the bedroom floor just before she opens the front door.

"Oh, hi – you seem sleepy. Have you slept all day?"

Her coat rustles when she gets down and picks the cat up.

"You're sweet when you're sleepy."

The sound of her high heels against the floor is almost deafening when she walks towards the chair. She bends down and moves the notebook. Then she sits down – the cat still in her arms. The living room is all quiet, except for the cat – purring so loud that the sound seems to fill the room. A long time passes before it frees itself from her and jumps onto the windowsill. She looks at it for a while, before noticing the amazing spectacle of the city roofs covered in white.

"How beautiful it is!"

She gets up to get a better view – a quiet smile spreading over her face. Then she nods and sits back down. She looks into the chair and finally finds the notebook that has slipped between the seat and the armrest. She quickly picks it up.

*Dear fifties*
*I have only seen the first half of you. You're exciting, but I don't really know what to do with you. I'm not quite finished with my forties yet – not at all, actually. I still feel young, but suddenly I'm middle aged. What to do with that expression? Middle aged is something you are when you're old or getting old. I am neither! So what to do with you? I expected a fabulous life, only to find out that it wasn't happening*

*– and certainly not without an effort. You have to create it yourself. There's no other way. But I don't know how to create a fabulous life.*

"Oh!"
A heavy sneeze makes the cat start.
"Sorry."
She laughs.
"But the weather today was devastating. I hope this isn't the start of a cold. I don't need that right now."
She sniffs a couple of times and then looks back at the notebook.

*And what is a fabulous life? After looking for the fabulous life I imagined for myself for many years, I am suddenly completely empty and without roots – confused about my entire life that just seems to have flown by. I always say that if time passes fast, it's because you're happy. Otherwise you would be aware of time and its many curious inputs. But when time is just gone, you've been happy. Time never passes more slowly than when you're unhappy – then it seems infinite and tiresome.*

*But feeling empty and confused in the middle of your life is a powerful experience. You think you're in control of everything, only to find out that you're actually not in control of anything at all. Damn it, what are you then if you can't even define yourself...? You have become so grown up that you no longer have anything to live up to. Total freedom – is that the fabulous life? Or is it just a symbol of emptiness and lack of relations with other people.*

*The fabulous life… Maybe it's just what you make of it. Or else it's a life with no regrets – which might actually be the ultimate happiness. Oh, I really don't know what I want from a fabulous life. What is fabulous anyway? That I can spend all that mon…*

The sound of breaking china interrupts the silence. She stares at the door to the hallway and then looks around the room.

"Where are you? Is that you?"

She gets up quickly and disappears out the door.

"Hmm, where are you?"

The cat answers her with a faint meow.

"Are you in the bedroom?"

She walks over to the bedroom.

"Come here you crazy bastard. Why have you been on the table? There was nothing but old food on that plate."

Together they walk back to the kitchen.

"Oh, you have no food left. Poor thing! Have I forgotten to feed you?"

The cat lands on the floor with a thump and soon the bag of cat food rustles.

"Some fresh water as well, then you should be all right."

It takes a while before she's back in the living room. She picks up the notebook and sits down.

*What has money got to do with a fabulous life?*

*Freedom, opportunities, what are they worth if you can't share them with someone? It's like being on a fabulous vacation... hmm, that word again... on a fabulous vacation and showing pictures afterwards to your friends. What a disappointment every time. The waterfall where you could feel a physical force pressing against your chest, the sound of the masses of water thundering into the deep – now reduced to a vertical streak of water running through lush, green surroundings. The person, who happens to stand next to the waterfall, doesn't matter to you and doesn't give you any idea of the actual size of the waterfall. He's probably not even that tall anyway. The fabulous is obliterated and it's only fabulous for the person who was actually there at that moment. But then it's not the picture that's fabulous, but the experience – the memory...*

*Some might say that I've had a fabulous life or maybe just a good life. But it didn't come without a price – relationships that have failed again and again, and the highest price of them all.*

She stops writing, but keeps the pen close to the paper.

*I lost my baby because I wanted to have it all. I didn't know how to listen to my body or to good advice from people around me. I didn't trust them to want the best for me. I thought I had my body under control like I had everything else in my life under control. But I didn't. The man of my life never forgave me, and I think he still hates me for it. I really thought I had everything under control. I usually run things, but somehow I had let things run me. I just stepped up the pace without thinking about it. One day my body couldn't take it anymore. I learned the hard way that I couldn't do everything at once. So it was over before it began. The little girl I should have shared the rest of my life with. It was over. Over!*

*What a terrible word. So final!*

Her body is shaking, and she puts the notebook down very carefully on the windowsill. Her eyes are once again locked on the orange cover.

"I still don't understand it. Even after ten years."

She gets up and stares out the window, rubs her eyes, and leaves the living room. The silence is loud, and the light remains off. The coffee machine starts making noises, and she pulls a chair over the kitchen floor. When the coffee machine is quiet again, she opens the cupboard and a heavy sound of china against wood comes from the kitchen. The chair makes a creaking sound.

It seems like the cat has finished eating, and it slurps some water almost without making a sound. But that sound goes away too, like the sounds from the neighbors. It's quiet. Even the sounds from the street have died down in the cold evening air that forms frostwork on the window with the bright street lights as background.

Finally, the sound of the cat's claws as it moves over the living room floor. It looks up at the windowsill for a long time before setting off and landing perfectly. It sits close to the window and its breath forms a small circle of moist when it hits the glass. Eyes and ears are intensely focused on what's happening down in the street.

The cat turns its head towards the kitchen and the chair that's once again creaking. The clear sound of china against the counter and the snorkeling of the coffee machine seem familiar to the cat. It yawns slowly and turns its attention back to the street. Her steps are slow and hesitant as they approach, and it takes a long time for her to reach the chair. She stands for a while, looking down at the seat that suddenly seems shabby to her. She looks down at the cat and drops into the chair.

*I found out because there was blood on my seat when I got up after the meeting. I love my job, and I hate my job. I love it because of what it makes me, but hate it for what it's done to me. I hate it for making me lonely for the rest of my life. I don't know any more if I have anybody in my life until the day I die. Like a daughter would have been there... Or am I just a hopeless romantic...? Oh, how should I know? I'm just a person – as incomplete as I was the day I was born. I'm even convinced that I will always be incomplete... Unfinished until the day I die.*

*I still remember the feeling of powerlessness, surrealism, when we had to choose the headstone. It was a mild spring day, but I was freezing. Our eyes met, but his showed only disgust. We hardly spoke when we picked the stone. We were too exhausted to argue about it. But it is beautiful. I remember I was nervous when I pulled out the little note from my pocket and gave it to him. Somehow I managed to say, "I want this to be on the stone." He took the piece of paper and looked at it for a long time – then he just nodded. "That's it, I suppose?" His voice was quivering, but I nodded my head and confirmed that the red, heart shaped stone was ordered and that it was OK to part. The result is beautiful. I'm still pleased every time I go to place some flowers. The golden letters against the red stone accentuate how I think her mind would have been – and the words "I died so I could live on" feel so right. She lives in my mind every day. I remember the journey home. I walked for over two hours. It looked like rain, it rained and then it cleared up before I came home. The stairs seemed endless and the front door heavier than ever before. The moment the front door closed behind me, I remember that I decided to buy my own grave site. I wanted to lie next to my daughter, and I still want that today. The ten years that have passed have changed nothing – not my feelings, not my mind or my thoughts. It's as if I haven't moved since that day. Life has moved on. I've changed, but when it comes to that, nothing has changed. It's just a little easier to live with.*

She puts down the pen and scratches her nose. Her breathing is fast. She looks at the cat and notices the round spot in the window in front of the cat's nose. The moon is surrounded by a halo – shining brightly in the frosty air. She puts the notebook down on the windowsill.

The cat turns its head and stares at it. It leans over and sniffs it but soon loses interest, and soon goes back to sitting with the nose close to the window. She stares straight ahead without noticing the cat. Then she pulls up her legs and rests her head on the back of the deep chair. She closes her eyes. After a while her breathing becomes slow and calm. The sound seems to affect the cat. It looks at her for a while before going back to sleep on its blanket.

For a long time, it's quiet as the moon moves over the clear, frosty night sky. The cat wakes up at some point, but this time it doesn't seem interested in what's happening down in the street. It stretches and yawns, watches her, and listens attentively to her breathing. Then it jumps down and walks slowly into the kitchen. The food bowl clatters as it slides over the floor and soon after you can hear the crunchy sound of the cat eating, and then the sound of paws against the bed sheets. Her breathing becomes shallower and she moves restlessly.

"No!"

She wakes with a start and suddenly sits upright in the chair. Her body is stiff and she stares around the living room. It takes a while before she can relax. She furrows her brow and falls back into the chair. She sighs and tries to see the time on her wrist watch, but it's too dark now that the moonlight no longer shines through the window. She stays like that for a long time before getting up and walking over to the window. Her breath is moist against the cold glass as she watches the bright shine of the frostwork. It contains all the colors of the rainbow, and it changes every time she moves her head a little and the light from the street lamps breaks differently. She looks down at her watch.

"Hmm, it's five in the morning. I guess there's no reason to go to bed."

She looks around.

"I might as well go to work."

She runs her hands through her long hair and yawns.

"Let's get going."

She disappears from the living room with the water glass and the old coffee cup – leaving behind only the dark, dried up puddle.

"Oh, there you are. You took the bed and I got the chair tonight. You like that, don't you?"

# CHAPTER 8

"Where are you?"

Her steps stop.

"Are you still asleep? And here I am, back early from work. Oh, there you are. Ha, you look like you're still sleeping."

She sits down on her heels to pet the cat, but it quickly gets enough of that and disappears into the bathroom, where the cat litter soon makes a creaking noise. She walks into the kitchen and fills its food bowl, and before long a happy crunching sound is heard as the cat starts eating. She throws off her shoes in the bedroom and soon the water is running in the shower.

It's quiet for a while before she sits down in the chair by the window with the notebook in her lap – humming. She picks up the pen from the windowsill.

"Oops, my hair is dripping. That's not good."

She quickly removes the drop of water from the

paper and puts her long, dark hair behind her ears. She looks down, but suddenly the cat lands in her lap, rubs its head against her hand and jumps over in the window, where the sun has an immediate effect on it. It blinks and lies down.

*It's as if people have tried to touch my soul all my life, but their fingertips could never quite reach. Something held them back... Was I that something? They reached out for me, but instinctively I stepped back and away from them every time. Why?*

A car door slams in the street and makes the cat lift its head and look out the window. It listens and its body is alert. But there are no more sounds. It lowers its head again and looks at her. She's facing the sun and she has a smile on her lips. The sun makes her wet hair shine and the blue bathrobe has fallen down over one shoulder. Her skin is smooth and shiny and tight over her bones. She starts to hum as the warm room and the sunbeams envelop her like an embrace. With care, the cat places its head on its paws and before long it breathes regularly once again. It's quiet for some time, before the snoring of the cat seems to pull her back to reality.

*Why? Was I scared? And if I was, what was I scared of? I have no answers, but something pulled me away. It wasn't a conscious act. I wasn't aware that I was doing it... But was I scared or just lazy? Did I not want to be disturbed in my practical and comfortable life? Did I not have the capacity to make room for other people and change my habits and my thoughts? Was I mentally lazy?*

*How will the future look? Do I choose it for myself, or is it created for me from the outside? Can I choose something else if I don't like it?*

*I want to live my life over again. I think I know now how it should be lived so I get the most out of it – a life with room for everything – myself, other people, children and love. The love that everybody yearns for but never knows quite how to describe. It's always described with words that don't say what it really is, but what the person describing it wants from it. Love is judged by everyone, and hard – not for what it really is, but for what we want it to be... or require it to be. Poor love, it can never make anyone happy... or only very few. And why are those few then happy?*

"Hmm, yes why?"

Her voice is low, almost a whisper, and it makes the cat turn its head away without waking up. She notices the shadows surrounding her – making heavy patterns and figures on the walls and the floor. She knows they will change as the sun falls towards the horizon, but she doesn't know how. She realizes that she's getting cold. She looks over at the window and sees that nearly half of the sun is already hidden behind the rooftops. She pulls up the bathrobe and closes it in the front. She sits quietly – watching the sun on its way towards nightfall. It's as if peace slowly fills her as the darkness gets denser and finally surrounds her completely.

In the dark window in front of her she suddenly sees a ray of light. She turns her head and sees the faint light in the hallway coming from the kitchen. It seems to draw her closer. She tilts her head a little, wondering why the light is on in the kitchen. She doesn't remember switching it on and stares into the hallway for a long time. The door to the street slams and she hears steps. She recognizes the voice of the woman upstairs, but a man is with her. She doesn't know his voice. She listens for the steps, and then hears how they stop at the door – the two people still talking, their voices cheerful. Then there's a click and the steps continue into the apartment above her. The steps stop just inside the door and she can hear shoes against the floor. Then it's quiet. She looks at the ceiling where she last heard the shoes. Then she hears the water upstairs being turned on. She lifts her eyebrows and the wrinkles in her forehead become deeper. Then she turns her wristwatch around and looks at it briefly.

*And why are they happy? Maybe they didn't expect so much. They didn't have Hollywood style dreams, but saw it as an adventure, and built something – looked at it, and then built some more. Oh, if I could solve this, I could make millions as a marriage counselor. That wouldn't be so bad.*

She smiles.

"Then we could live in a huge house at a fancy

address, be admired by everyone, and photographed for the magazines. For something that everyone should be able to do and that no one should be denied."

She shakes her head.

"It should be for everybody and not just for the few…"

*Who is really rich when you think about it?*

*The couple, who have stayed together for 60 years, fought their way through life and the challenges it sent their way. They stood together, determined to overcome whatever was hiding in the nooks and corners of life. Or is it really the money that matters?*

*Why don't we ever say, "How rich they are", when we meet people who have lived out their dreams and desires? Why don't we admire them? At most we envy them… Maybe we will admire them if they have done something others wouldn't survive. Maybe it's worth admiring that they have survived, but should they have done it in the first place if it could have cost them their lives? Weren't they just being selfish and without any consideration for what they did to their loved ones and people who cared about them?*

She pulls the bathrobe tight around herself, tightens the belt, and once again puts her hair behind her ears. She picks up the reluctant cat – placing it on its back in her arms as she walks through the living room while talking to herself. She switches on the light in the hallway and then opens the fridge door.

"Hey, don't go anywhere. I know you have eaten already, but I have bought shrimps, so I think you would like a few before I eat them all myself."

The plastic lid on the box makes a creaking sound, and the cat answers with a loud, piercing meow.

"I thought so."

The sounds in the kitchen continue for a long time, and when she's back in the living room, she has changed and is ready to go. The skirt clings to her bottom and her thighs. She smoothes it a little and runs a hand through her still damp hair. Her eyes rest pensively on the notebook, while she breathes heavily – relaxed. She picks up the notebook and stands there like she's trying to weigh it in her hand. She cautiously scratches her right eye, careful not to smear the make-up. Then she puts the notebook down on the windowsill and picks up the pen. She bends over the book and starts writing.

*I want to swap my life. I have tried, but they don't give you any rights to do that when you're born. Life is given to you, and you must work with what you have. You are on your own. No matter how many good people you have in your life, you're always alone in the hardest moments with the toughest choices...*

*And the choices have been hard – maybe one of them still stands as the hardest. I don't know if I would have chosen differently today. I think I would have. But back then, things were as they were. I was in my twenties, had just met him and was deeply in love.*

*But when the consequences of things were clear to us, none of us could see the road ahead. The road was always there – right in front of us. But we couldn't see it. AND nobody could convince us that it was actually there. So the choice became a question of not choosing. Did I forgive myself in the meantime? Hmm, I actually don't know if I did. It's still deeply entrenched in me, that if only I had done a little more, everything might have turned out differently. Maybe we could have stayed at my parents' place... given it up for adoption... but the truth is that even today, I just don't know if it would have made a difference. Maybe I will never know – maybe that's the truth I have to live with.*

*I would like to have spent my twenties differently, but how? I really can't answer that. I only know the road I chose, and therefore only the result I live now.*

*Yes, that's the truth and the reality. Maybe I wanted to spend my twenties differently, but then how would my forties and fifties have been. They wouldn't be how I know them now.*

*I wonder if we are all given the same amount of good and bad in life. It's only a question of how we handle that. Would our lives be easier if this was a known fact – a label given to us at birth? So that the only unknown factor is that we don't know when we will be hit by the good and the bad. That's all we need to relate to – uncertainty.*

Her outline against the window looks like someone that could be in a commercial. The skirt hugs her bottom perfectly. She stands with her legs crossed, so that her heels touch each other perfectly, and the seams on her stockings are straight as arrows on their way up her long legs. She moves a little, so that her patent leather heels rub against each other – making a loud, creaking sound.

*But we're so bad at living with the uncertainty. So how would that help us? Deep down we all want certainty, safety and harmony... that is until we start to get bored...*

She slams the notebook shut and stands up straight. She smiles as her eyes look out over the white, snow covered scenery outside. The sound of her high heels stops in the bathroom and a weak puff is heard before a flowery smell spreads into the living room and a small laughter is heard.

"So sweetie, you don't like my new scent, I see. You've never left the bathroom that fast before."

The cat sits in the hallway – looking into the bathroom. Her steps continue down the hallway and the cupboard door is opened. You can clearly hear the sound of the coat sliding in place around her.

"Well, honey, I have to hurry. The girls are waiting for me by now."

Her voice is almost playful as she continues.

"Well! Girls!? We're all over fifty, but no one says no to a nice dinner. Uh, I'll be late. Have fun baby girl. See you later."

The sounds from the street are getting quieter as the rush hour subsides, and all at once, the street is quiet. It's as if the snow that has fallen during the day – and has started falling again – muffles the sounds once more. The sound of the snowplow is heard often during the night. The light from the outside seems to fade gradually as the snow increases. A sudden, out of place sound from the street – a voice, unintelligible, but alarming – and then a hollow sound. Suddenly everything is eerily quiet. Inquiring voices are heard from the street. It's a man and a woman. A muffled scream comes from the woman.

"My phone! My phone!"

His voice is mechanical and strangely void of feeling. The cat has gotten up and now sits very close to the window – its face and ears following every movement and every sound in the street below.

The man's voice is so weak that you can't make out the words. It's quiet, and then you can hear the woman's voice, which has a higher pitch.

"Are they on their way?"

More voices are heard from the street until the glaring sound of sirens drowns them all. The window is lit by the blinking lights and the figure of the cat is black behind the window. It's quiet both inside and outside. The blinking lights throw the shadows in the living room around, as if they're dancing over the walls and the floor. Another siren cuts through the silence below, and the living room is once again lit up by blinking lights, but this time the shadows keep dancing. Car doors slam, voices talk fast and in short sentences, but the words are unclear. Then it's quiet again. Another car arrives and new voices are heard. But silence returns – and seems to last. Then the sound of the ambulance door and soon after the sound of wheels that make the ice on the road creak. The blinking lights are less intense. Two voices fill the emptiness, then another door is closed and the lights in the living room dim into twilight. The ice creaks again, and the sound of the engine slowly fades.

Once again the living room is dark and the snow no longer fills the sky. A voice comes through with a calming tone.

"Go home."

The snowplow waits in one end of the street. Another car door slams and the ice gives a little. Soon after, the snowplow drives by the window. The silence is oppressive. The cat walks back and forth in the window and sits down to watch – its face very close to the window. It sits there without moving and the circle of moist slowly gets bigger.

The street door opens. Loud voices are talking and steps are noisy against the stairs. The door closes, but the voices don't hesitate. The steps continue to the first floor only, and then they disappear as the door closes behind them. Then it's quiet. The cat sits there, petrified, looking out the window as the waning moon moves across the sky. Slowly, light returns, and the cat seems to finally wake up. It jumps carefully down from the window and walks into the kitchen, only to return without any success. The food bowl is still empty.

# CHAPTER 9

Light chases away the last of the darkness, and the day is gray and sad outside the window. The change in the weather started as the night began, and has resulted in dripping gutters and has also melted away the white edge in front of the window. The paperboy unlocks the door to the staircase and walks quietly up to the fifth floor – the newspaper hits the floor hard. Then he quietly walks down the stairs again. The first rays from the sun come through late in the day, and reach the cat that's still sitting close to the window. It just sits there without moving. It only moves the eyes. The sun hits the cat with full strength when at last it breaks free from the clouds just over the horizon. The cat finally moves away slowly, and another trip to the food bowl ends without fulfilling its purpose. Clear, metallic sounds from the kitchen can be heard as the food bowl hits the wall. Steps are heard in the staircase and the door to the street closes hard. The house is quiet. The first neighbors have come home, and the children are already playing. Then the sound of the key in the lock is heard. The cat runs quickly into the hallway and sits in front of the door just before it opens.

"There you are."

The cat backs away when it sees the stranger, but then it hurries over to her leg and rubs its head against it. The voice is slow and hesitant and strange to the cat. But hunger seems to have taken over.

"Have you been all alone? Are you hungry?"

She strokes its head and it starts to purr.

"Come along, and you can have some food before we leave."

She disappears into the kitchen with the cat close on her heels. Cupboards are opened and closed quickly, and the cat answers with a persistent series of loud meows. When the food hits the food bowl, the purring gets almost unnaturally loud. The metal makes a noise when she puts the food bowl back on the floor. The cat crunches the food. Another metallic sound follows.

"Here's some fresh water as well, so you don't have to drink the old water."

The crunchy sound of the food stops and the cat starts to purr again.

"You just eat, and I will have a look around in the meantime."

Steps move around the apartment, and soon the tall, slender figure in worn-out jeans and a much too big, red sweater arrives in the living room. She stands close to the window – looking down as she removes some strands of long, blond hair from her face. Tears roll down her cheeks. She turns away and lets her eyes move around the living room while drying the tears away with her sleeve.

The orange cover of the notebook lights up in the final rays from the sun, and her eyes stop there. She picks it up and turns it around in her hands, before she lets her hand slide over the surface and feels the tickling feeling against it. She closes her hand and rubs her fingers against each other to get rid of the feeling. She looks around the living room again, before slowly sitting down in the green armchair – almost as if she's afraid to sit in it. Finally she lets herself fall back in it completely and rests her back. She looks at the notebook and then looks away. She lets her left hand run over the green chair – feeling the flowery scent that still hangs in the room. Her right hand rests on the notebook in her lap. Finally she looks down and opens it.

*The golden letters against the red stone accentuate how I think her mind would have been – and the words "I died so I could live on" feel so right. She lives in my mind every day.*

She reads almost unnaturally slow. Suddenly she hears the weak sound of a tear hitting the paper of the notebook. She wipes it away carefully and closes the notebook again, putting it back on the windowsill. She looks at it for a long time before pushing it in a little further, as if she's afraid it will fall down.

"I wonder if you will also get a red stone with golden letters – and with the same epitaph."

She breathes heavily.

"But you will definitely lie next to Emma. You made sure of that."

She starts as the cat jumps onto the windowsill to stand close to the window again, looking down. She didn't hear it coming.

"My, you are quiet. I'll have to get used to that."

She looks at it as it slowly sits down without taking its eyes off the street below. She gets up and looks down. Her eyes fill with tears again. She tenderly lifts the cat down from the window.

"Let's find your pet carrier, and then we'll go out and buy some new stuff for you. We won't bring any of the old stuff. We'll start over at my place."

She tilts her head.

"I have never heard your name. Do you have a name?"

She strokes its head and her hand touches the collar. She turns over the little name tag that's shaped like a cat's head.

"Emma."

She carefully forms the word, and there's a note of surprise in her voice.

"I didn't expect that. I really didn't."

She looks into the street one last time – taking care that the cat can't look down there again. She hugs it before walking into the hallway holding it in her arms. Cupboards are opened and closed and then the sound of drawers is heard. It's finally quiet.

"I didn't know you had such a nice bag. It's got little cats on it. Do you want to get in there?"

It's quiet for a moment.

"That didn't take you long. Well, then this is your travel bag. I can see that you're ready. Wait a second."

Fast steps down the hallway and over the floor of the living room.

"I think this is for me."

She picks up the notebook, looks around and nods.

"Now it's time."

The twilight creeps in through the window and the furniture begins to form shadows. The steps hurry away from the window and stop shortly when she picks up the bag with the cat and throws it over her shoulder. It's quiet as the snowplow passes again down in the street. The ice on the road has given in to the thaw a long time ago, and the sound of asphalt against iron is heard regularly.

"It's time."

She puts the notebook down on the small shelf next to the front door – trying to close her jacket without putting down the cat.

"It's weird that this is both the first and the last time I'll ever visit my aunt's apartment. Somebody will come tomorrow to clear it. I am not allowed to do that, but they don't really want to... They just want it done quickly, so they don't have to pay an extra month's rent."

She nods.

"But at least they let me pick you up… Emma."

She looks down and her eyes meet the cat's – sitting calmly in the bottom of the bag looking up at her. She nods.

"Are you Emma?"

Her voice is cheerful, and the cat answers her with a meow. She laughs.

"You ARE an Emma."

The front door closes and her steps disappear down the stairs. The door to the street closes heavily, and it's quiet again. A loud snap is heard when the orange notebook hits the floor.

# ABOUT THE AUTHOR

Tina Lindegaard was born in 1963 when the world lost its innocence with the murder of John F. Kennedy, and when a song became the symbol of one man's dream that became the dream of thousands.

Tina Lindegaard was born in a provincial town in Denmark and spent her first 20 years in a small town where nature was never far away. She moved to Copenhagen, which is still her home. Her character is formed by the natural surroundings of her childhood, and a busy career that has not always been in tune with her upbringing. These contrasts have created a field of tension with lots of room for creativity, and formed a multi-faceted view of human nature.

You can follow the author and learn more about upcoming books on Twitter and read her blog via **www.MouseJournal.com**.